C000154919

Claiming Jafar

Fairytales After Dark

Astrid Vail

Claiming Jafar

Copyright © 2022 by Astrid Vail & Rogue Queen Publishing

All rights reserved.
No part of this book may be used or reproduced, stored or transmitted in any
form or by any means, electronic, mechanical, photocopying, recording,
scanning, or otherwise in any manner whatsoever without written permission
except in the case of brief quotations bodied in critical articles or reviews.

It is illegal to copy this book, post it on a website, or distribute it by any means without
permission.

This book is a work of fiction. Names, characters, businesses, organizations, places, events, and incidents either are the product of the author's imagination or are used
fictitiously. Any resemblance to actual persons, living or dead, events, or locales is entirely coincidental.

Cover Art by https://www.getcovers.com
Edited by https://www.nicegirlnaughtyedits.com

ISBN:

eBook: 978-1-958641-00-2

Paperback: 978-1-958641-11-8

First Edition: September 2022

CW: This story contains on page sexual acts, violence, infidelity and language.

Contents

Blurb and Content Warning

He wants her power, and her heart.
Never in her wildest dreams did Jasmine think she would
be ruling her kingdom by herself as her happily ever
after spills from her hands like sand through an hourglass.
Finding her kingdom on the brink of ruin, she turns to the
one man who can help her locked away for his traitorous
crimes.
Yet, Jafar's ruthlessness might be the one thing Jasmine
needs to help her kingdom. In desperate need of council,
she is willing to meet his demands and in doing so,
Jasmine just might become the ruler her kingdom always
needed.
And the one Jafar always wanted.
*This is a M/F, erotic enemies to lover's novella between
consenting adults.*
Content Warning: This book contains graphic sexual
scenes, language, violence, and infidelity.

Chapter One

THE SLAP OF FLESH permeated the room, pre-dawn light trickling in through gauzy curtains. A soft breeze filtered in, caressing Jasmine's face. She glanced towards the open balcony and scowled. *Damn it*, she thought. She still needed to bathe, get dressed, and become presentable before the emissaries from the Northern Territories came knocking on the palace doors. And

Aladdin was taking his sweet time getting off this morning. She needed to finish this. Plus, her leg was cramping from holding it in this position for so long. Stretching out her arm, Jasmine grabbed Aladdin's bare ass and gave it a hard squeeze, sinking her nails into his soft flesh. She faked a high-pitched groan, but Aladdin was oblivious as he grunted, plowing into her harder. Two short, furious strokes later, he finally came. Jasmine let out a sigh of relief as he rolled off her, a satisfied grin encompassing his face. "Pre-morning sex is the best sex. Isn't it, Princess Jassie."

"Sultanah..." Jasmine mumbled, not even addressing the stupid play on her name he had started using. Aladdin sat up and stretched, before flopping back down onto the strewn about pillows. He frowned as Jasmine got up and put on her robe.

"What's the rush? I'll be ready for round two soon."

Jasmine glanced down her nose at the man she had fought tooth and nail to get, to have her father's approval of, along with her whole country, and felt nothing but contempt. "We have a meeting with the emissaries from the Northern Territories this week. Or did you forget?"

Aladdin groaned and waved Jasmine off. "You are better at that stuff than I am. You can do this without me. And if you are going to be busy for the rest of the day, then I'm going into the city."

Jasmine huffed and folded her arms, the move pushing her tits up. She could tell the sight was appetizing by the way Aladdin's gaze dipped and the disgusting way he licked his upper lip. He lifted his eyes, pleading like a dog in heat, and Jasmine shook her head. If she was to be presentable as the Sultanah of her land by the time the emissaries arrived, she had to leave at once. "Don't spend too much money at the bar this time. The guards had to carry you home two nights in a row, and it isn't..." She struggled for a nice word, before saying, "Dignified."

Aladdin had the audacity to look shocked, brows scrunching together, and lips parted. "That isn't a nice thing to say to your husband, Jassie."

"It's just an observation, Aladdin. And I would like you to join me at the meetings today."

He settled into a pout that could rival that of any pampered child, and Jasmine gave up, throwing her hands in the air. "Fine. Do whatever you want. I'm not going to argue about this. I have a country to run."

Aladdin scoffed as Jasmine turned from him but stopped short at the tight grip on her shoulder. "Don't be upset with me, Jassie. I was a thief and a beggar before this, living on the streets my whole life. I don't know any of this political rulership stuff. You married me because you loved me, remember? And this is me."

Jasmine let out a long-winded sigh and pinched the bridge of her nose between her fingers. "I just need you to try a little harder, okay? The emissaries from the Northern Territories are used to seeing men occupying the throne, not a female. It just makes things harder from the start. At least sit by my side for half the day."

Aladdin conceded, letting go of her shoulder, and huffing a dramatic, "Fine."

That was all she needed for the time being. *I hope he doesn't run his mouth at the meeting,* Jasmine thought as she took off towards the palace bathing rooms. Aladdin acting the fool was the last thing she needed for the start of these important negotiations.

ALADDIN DID INDEED RUN his mouth... all the way to the opium den by mid-day, along with part of the emissary's entourage. "Well, Jasmine..." she murmured to herself, head dipping low over the table in front of her, "you did tell him not to go to the bar. So this was obviously your fault." She picked up a small figurine on the map before her and moved it across invisible lines into another territory. Letting out a sigh, Jasmine rubbed the back of her neck and glanced outside. The sun had set, casting an eerie, fiery glow across the expanse of desert before her. The city lit up like a beacon, shadows slowly descending their way down stark white exteriors. Jasmine padded out onto the balcony silently, leaning over the stone balustrade to take in the view.

Hers. This was hers.

It was everything she ever wanted. To rule her people with kindness, compassion, and with a competent ruler by her side. Not some boy masquerading as a man. Jasmine turned her back on the glowing city below and gripped the barrier behind her, letting her head fall back to watch the stars as they lit up the sky. Shaking her head, she wished there was a way to make Aladdin understand he couldn't be an absentee ruler. Here she was, wishing on the stars, like a little naïve girl. Something she no longer was. Running this city by herself without an advisor on her side was slowly eating her alive. She was in desperate need of help.

Her stomach clenched at the thought, but she knew what had to be done. She had officially run out of options. Running fingers through her loose hair, Jasmine began piling it atop her head. Marching back into the room, she snatched up her discarded hair pins and aggressively shoved them into place. They scraped at her scalp, but she didn't care. The pain centered her. As she grabbed her discarded crown, Jasmine turned towards her full-length mirror before placing it on her head. She took in the wrinkles of her long decorative tunic and high-waisted skirts. They were heavy and cumbersome but expected of a female on the throne. Jasmine had no idea why she hadn't summoned a worker to help her change hours ago. Ignoring the itchy red welt on her collarbone caused by the tunic's fabric, she instead took a deep breath, steeling her spine for what was about to come. Flicking a piece of stray hair out of her face, Jasmine turned and marched out of her quarters. She would need all the confidence in her armory for the person she was about to speak to.

The scum of all that was holy, but... he was the only person Jasmine knew of who was conniving enough to help her through these negotiations. The only one who could help her city from succumbing to the tides of war.

Jafar.

Chapter Two

JASMINE SUCKED IN A breath, hesitating before the dungeon door. She had her gaze on the handle, hand reaching out, when the guard on duty cleared his throat. "Princess?"

Jasmine turned, about to tell the guard off, before she regained her composure and took in a calming breath. "Open the door... Please." The guard looked around, as if searching for someone, and Jasmine cocked her head. "Who are you looking for?"

The guard shook his head. "Is it just you?"

Jasmine gave the guard a hard look and leaned back on her heels. "Is that a problem for you?"

The guard quickly shook his head and shoved a key into the lock. "Sorry, Princess. The prisoner is shackled and chained to the wall. Do you need an escort?"

Jasmine shook her head as the guard pulled the door open for her. "Thank you," she murmured before stepping over the threshold into the dimly lit dungeon. The flickering light from the low burning torches greeted her, and Jasmine wrinkled her nose at the pungent smell of filth filtering through the air. A deep, rasping laugh echoed throughout the chamber, and Jasmine's upper lip curled. "Is something funny, Jafar?"

As Jasmine's eyes become accustomed to the dim light, they caught movement on the far wall. A disheveled man with wild hair tumbling over his shoulders and a beard in desperate need of a cut raised his head, torch light flickering to give his dark amber brown eyes a devilish glow. "Just laughing at the little girl standing in front of me, who has the audacity to call herself Sultanah of this great city."

Jasmine's sharp inhale echoed throughout the dungeon, and Jafar released another rasping laugh. "It was a mistake coming here." She shook her head, before turning on her heel. She would just have to figure this out another way.

"So you just came down here to let me hurl insults at you?"

Jasmine stopped in her tracks and glanced over her shoulder. "And that is all you will ever be capable of doing because from where I'm standing, all I see is some two-faced jackal has-been who chased power over loyalty and found himself locked away in a dungeon."

Jafar barked in laughter. "Close, little girl, but still not a hit."

Jasmine turned fully, rage building low in her chest. She was getting sick and tired of people not respecting her title. Most of the time, she brushed it off, wanting her people like her, but the man sitting in front of her... she couldn't care less.

"I am your Sultanah, and you will address me as such."

Jafar's lips turned up into a sinister grin. "Such prickly words, my Sultanah. Why do you bestow them upon me, yet not your guard?"

Jasmine sucked in a harsh breath and leveled her stare at Jafar. "I am not here for your opinions on how I allow my people to address me. I am here for something else."

Jafar raised an eyebrow and slowly leaned forward, coming first to his knees before standing. Jasmine's eyes flickered up, taking in his imposing form. He was filthy, disheveled, and skinnier than when he first landed himself in the dungeons, and yet... he never lost his presence. Jafar had always radiated confidence and... Jasmine's thoughts stuttered when she met his eyes. Rolling back her shoulders, she scowled, wishing she had the same natural confidence as this traitor standing before her.

"And what exactly are you here for? To gloat? To apologize? To get a good fuck?"

Jasmine's mouth fell open at Jafar's last words. "What did you just say to me?"

"I said... do you need a good fuck?"

Jasmine bristled, anger flushing her cheeks as she strode forward, hand rising. She was tired of the disrespect and at least here, she could punish the insubordination.

The slap echoed, flesh hitting flesh. Jafar's low growl slid down Jasmine's spine, making her shiver. He slowly turned his head, tongue flicking out to catch the drop of blood swelling upon his lower lip. His eyes burned with anger and Jasmine's breath hitched, realizing how close she was to him, their chests barely an inch away. She had made a big mistake. His movement was fast, one hand snaking around the back of her neck, tangling in the nape of her hair, and the other coming up to squeeze her jaw. Fear skittered behind Jasmine's eyes, and she knew this was it. Jafar was about to snap her neck. Her rule would fall to an incompetent man-child more concerned about extravagance than her country. Jafar leaned in, towering over her, and she struggled to speak. To try to plead for him not to kill her, but his grip on her jaw was too strong as he tilted her head back. Fingernails bit into Jasmine's scalp as Jafar yanked down, her neck screaming at the sudden movement. Jafar had full control over her in this moment, and Jasmine's stomach dipped as he leaned down to whisper into her ear, "That was a mistake. Think of this as a teachable moment. Never... *ever* let your emotions take your control away from you."

With those final words, Jafar released his grip, pushing her away roughly. Jasmine barely kept to her feet, stumbling, and almost falling. Her hand shook as she grazed the slightly raised skin along her jaw. That fucking bastard.

Jafar blinked slowly before sitting back down and leaning against the wall. He began picking at the dirt under his nails, completely ignoring her. "We are done here."

His dismissal chaffed at Jasmine's skin, and she dropped her hand. "You are a vile, treacherous leech of a man. I should have you executed immediately for touching me."

Jafar sighed with a shrug. "Then do it. I tire of being in this disgusting dungeon. Kill me or find a use for me. I don't care which. Go speak to your father and council about it. I'll wait."

Tears threatened Jasmine's eyes immediately at the mention of her father and she swiftly turned away, giving Jafar her back. "I can't." The words fell from her lips as a forlorn whisper, but Jafar heard them, nonetheless. Chains rattled, filling the silent dungeon briefly with noise as if begging to be acknowledged, but Jasmine couldn't make herself look at him. She couldn't let her tears fall. Not in his presence. "He rests within the shrine now and my council abandoned me months ago." Jasmine took a step, moving towards the stairs, before Jafar's sigh stopped her.

"You have been running your country by yourself, then?"

She lifted a shoulder, deciding to tell him the truth. Jasmine didn't know why the words fell from her mouth, but they did. "Yes, and I need help. I need your help, Jafar. I seek council."

His chains rattled once more, and she finally turned, facing him head on. The traitor who tried to take the kingdom away from her father. The villain who she was asking help from to keep her country from falling to ruin. Jasmine expected a lecherous smirk, a face conveying unbridled joy. Yet instead, as his eyes met hers, all Jasmine saw was rage. Jafar sneered, "If I am to be your council, my Sultanah, then I have a few requests. And the first one is releasing me from these shackles."

Chapter Three

JASMINE WORRIED AT HER nail, staring out into the dim sky through a small window. She lingered in the corridor, not even knowing why. Her palms were wet with perspiration, thoughts going back to who and what she just conceded to. Jafar had made requests... requests Jasmine couldn't think of a reason not to give in to.

They were reasonable, beyond reasonable if he was going to offer council. One of the requests was leaving the dungeon and getting a room on the same floor as hers. When Jasmine said absolutely not without the presence of the guards, he had given her a look. *Of course, I will have guards on my person at all times, my Sultanah. You are not that incompetent.*

He had also requested a bath at once... and a lover for the night. Jasmine had almost balked at his last request and the way his eyes roamed her body. As if she was the lover he wanted. His words after the look echoed in her mind. *Don't worry, I don't want you in my bed. You wouldn't be able to satiate my appetite anyway.*

Jasmine's face warmed as his words played in her memory and then from the noises coming from behind the door she stood next to. This was the second time she had passed by. She had awoken hours ago, panic-stricken that Jafar had made his escape somehow and had stolen her throne. Rushing from her bed in only her robe, Jasmine ran to the throne room, only for it to be blissfully empty. Seeing how it was still night, morning light hours away, she along walked her empty palace corridors. Taking in the quiet serenity... until she passed by Jafar's room and the moans resonating out from under the door. Jasmine's face had flushed, and she rushed away. Only to find herself once more outside Jafar's door, as dawn starting to make its ascent, and he was still at it. She briefly wondered if he had more than one lover and if this was the same round as before. Then Jasmine's stomach pinched in worry as she noticed the guards were nowhere in sight. Were they in the room with him?

Jasmine raised her hand and knocked. The sounds inside picked up pace, and Jasmine scowled, knocking harder. The door creaked open to reveal the face of a flustered guard, thankfully fully dressed. "Yes, Princess?" he whispered, and Jasmine plastered a fake smile on her face.

"I need to speak to Jafar once he is decent. Today's meeting with the emissaries is in a few hours." At her words, the noises ceased, and the door opened all the way. The man who looked back at her was no longer dirty, though just as disheveled, but in a very different way. The tips of his curly hair scraped against his collarbones, and as he brought his hand up to shove his hair out of his eyes, Jasmine gulped at the sight of his naked chest. Sweat glistened across his skin, and when her eyes finally made their way to his face, they snagged on his full lips before meeting amber brown eyes. They were just as dark and devilish as they had been in the dungeon, and Jasmine was glad. It reminded her that even washed and groomed, Jafar was still the same man who had landed himself in the dungeon. Looking over his shoulder, her eyes widened as she took in not one but three naked women in his bed. Jafar cleared his throat and Jasmine's eyes snapped back to his face. "Do you request council for the day?"

Jasmine nodded. "Yes. I will need you by my side with the Northern Emissary in a few hours. I thought we should speak strategy."

Jafar turned and pointed to the women still sprawled out in his bed. "Out now. Your Sultanah needs to speak to her advisor."

Jasmine opened her mouth to protest that she could wait, but Jafar leveled a look at her, making her mouth snap shut. The three women rushed out in various stages of undress, not even acknowledging her presence. Jafar's lips flushed together in a grim line, but he didn't say anything. Instead, he stepped away, giving Jasmine room and beckoned her inside. Nodding to the guards, she pointed to the door. "You may wait right outside."

The guards looked at her, then to Jafar. "Princess, I do not—"

Jasmine scowled, mouth opening to cut him off, but it was not her voice that rolled through the room.

"Address your Sultanah by her proper title."

She glanced at Jafar, surprised at his interjection and the furious look crossing his face. The guards hesitated, glancing between the two of them. "Apologies, Sultanah, but I do not think it is wise to leave you alone with the prisoner."

Jasmine steadied her voice, putting resolve behind her command. "Leave. Now."

The guard's jaw ticked, and he glanced at Jafar once more before turning on his heel and leaving. Jasmine shut the door behind him and took in Jafar, now lounging at the small sitting table next to the open balcony. He popped a date into his mouth before leveling a stare in her direction. "You have a problem with insubordination, my Sultanah."

Jasmine lifted her chin and stalked over to the open chair, but didn't sit. "It is a work in progress. They are used to me being the princess."

Jafar shrugged. "Might I suggest a few beheadings. They will learn quickly to call you by your title. They will also follow your orders when given."

Jasmine paused, blinking at the man in front of her before sitting at the small table. "I do not wish to rule through fear, Jafar. I will not stoop to your level."

Jafar chuckled before popping another date into his mouth. "I hope you do not mind. I am famished. It was a... long night."

Jasmine shook her head and tried not to look at the rumpled bed behind Jafar. "I do not mind. Now for the Northern Emissary... unfortunately, it has not been the best of starts."

Jafar turned his devilish eyes her way. "Tell me how it has gone so far. Then we will figure out the best course of action for today."

She took a deep breath. "It has been difficult to sit in negotiations as a lone female ruler. I do not want the trade agreements to cease, but it seems to be whenever I am in the presence of other rulers or negotiations are taking place, I am dismissed, not an equal in their eyes. So, to prevent this, I sought to have Aladdin sit in on the meetings. Sometimes just the presence of a man can help negotiations run smoothly."

Jasmine paused, waiting for Jafar to say something. Instead, he popped another date into his mouth and waited, eyes never wavering from her face. "Aladdin can be problematic sometimes. He has chosen not to..." Jasmine hesitated once more, trying to find a relatively nice word to describe her husband's actions.

Jafar didn't seem to have her same qualms. "He acts like a child? He just wants to play and doesn't care about ruling a country? Tell me what he has done."

"He calls me pet names in front of the emissaries, tells stories of his days living on the streets, and last night, he took half the delegation out to the opium dens. The rest left to their rooms under the impression that my rulership is a sham, and my kingdom is an easy target. I fear it will start with a loss of the trade agreements and eventually invasion. I don't want to go to war. I just want peace."

Jafar slowly let out a breath, and Jasmine's eyes roamed his face, looking for anything to give away what he was thinking. Nothing peeked through his indifferent exterior. "Your kingdom *is* an easy target."

"Excuse me?" Jasmine stood, fury flushing her face as she leaned over the table and glared at Jafar.

"Do you remember my first lesson? Or do I need to remind you." He stood as he spoke, their faces coming within inches of each other. Jasmine's breath hitched, and she had a wild thought that if they just closed the distance by a hairsbreadth, they would be having a completely different conversation. Fortunately, a commotion of words beyond the doors interrupted Jasmine's insane thought, and she moved. Jafar was quick to follow. Ripping open the doors, she stepped into the hallway, only to find Aladdin stumbling down them, singing as loudly as he could with a bottle of liquor in his hand. At his side was the head of the Northern Emissary, just as drunk as her husband. Aladdin spotted her and his eyes widened. He pointed to her, then Jafar, mouth going slack. "What... are... *what?*"

Jasmine rolled her eyes and strode forward, taking Aladdin by the arm. "Come on. Let's get you to our room." Normally complacent, Jasmine didn't anticipate Aladdin ripping his arm from her grasp as he pointed to Jafar again. "Are you fucking him? He is a traitor and tried to kill me!"

Jasmine gaped at Aladdin before it dawned on her. Jafar was still disheveled from a night spent with three women, and still only dressed in a thin pair of sleeping pants. And all she was wearing was her robe. "Aladdin. Of course not. Let us discuss this in our quarters."

Aladdin scoffed but turned, making his way down the hall and slamming into the door of their quarters before yanking it open and stumbling inside. Taking a deep breath, Jasmine acknowledged the head of the Northern Emissary. "Do we need to push our meeting to later?"

He glanced at her, eyes roving Jasmine's body in a lecherous way. "I suggest speaking to your husband. We came to an agreement about your kingdom late last night."

Jasmine's spine went rigid. "My husband does not have a say in the final proceeding of my kingdom. I will speak to him and push our meeting to later this evening."

Stalking towards her chambers, Jasmine took a deep breath and pushed the doors open. As she turned to close them, she caught sight of Jafar staring her down, with a look Jasmine could only take as resentment and ire flashing briefly across his face.

Closing the doors, Jasmine pondered why Jafar would feel resentment in that moment, but that was something to figure out later. For now, it was time to confront Aladdin and the damage he had inflicted upon her negotiations with the Northern Emissaries.

Chapter Four

JASMINE LET LOOSE A low sigh before turning and looking for Aladdin. He was sitting on the floor, back against the bed. He lifted the bottle to his lips and pointed to the now closed door. "What is *he* doing out of the dungeon?"

Jasmine shook her head and took a step forward, trying to take the bottle from his hands. Aladdin jerked away and slid, his back hitting the floor with a thud. He laid there, staring at the ceiling. "Why don't you love me anymore, Jasmine?"

His whisper had tears forming at the corners of her eyes and Jasmine padded forward, sitting beside him on the cool stone floor. "Aladdin, look at me." He turned his head, gaze unfocused and hazy. Jasmine reached out, smoothing away the stray hairs covering his eyes. "I do love you. I just need council. I am drowning at court. It has become too much. I am alone on the throne, and I am running this kingdom by myself. I need help."

Aladdin struggled to sit up, and Jasmine helped, pulling him into a sitting position. "That's why I took the emissary out. I gave him the kingdom. You don't have to worry anymore."

Jasmine felt all the blood drain from her face as his words resonated in her mind. "You don't have the authority to do that, Aladdin. My name is on the documents. I am the one who took the throne, not you."

Aladdin waved his hand about, alcohol splashing to the floor from the bottle he still held. "But I am your husband. They do not acknowledge female rulers. I did this for us. Now we can stay in bed all day. They will take care of everything."

Jasmine slid her hand from his and stood, taking a step back. "I can't believe you did this. You have muddled up these negotiations. Do you not realize what you have done?" Jasmine worried at her nail, glancing around. "How am I going to fix this?"

Aladdin surged up from the floor and wobbled over to the open balcony. "Are you saying you choose your kingdom over me?" He motioned to the city laid out before them.

Jasmine shook her head in confusion. "What are you talking about? You are drunk. You need to lie down and sleep this off."

Aladdin shook his head and took a staggering step towards her. "No. I will not let you take all of this away from me. The agreement I made will leave us at the palace. We just have to do what they say."

Jasmine shook her head once more, not understanding what she was hearing. This was the most inebriated she had ever seen Aladdin, and he was making absolutely no sense.

She stood, reaching out, pity lacing her words. "Aladdin—" The bottle flew, connecting with her shoulder, then shattered as it hit the desk next to her. The sound of glass breaking filled Jasmine's shocked mind, and she took a step back, slipping on the wet floor. She fell with a thud, taking the chair next to the desk down with her.

Jasmine stared at her husband in shock as Aladdin's face hardened and he rushed forward, hands reaching. On instinct alone, she scrambled away, only then realizing what was happening. Aladdin managed to grab one of her ankles, dragging her back. "Jasmine! I will not go back to living on the streets. I will make you sign that agreement with the Northern Emissary if I have to."

Aladdin reached for her other ankle and pulled them both back towards the bed and Jasmine twisted, rolling onto her stomach and breaking Aladdin's hold. She didn't look back as she scrambled to her hands and knees, hearing Aladdin's startled grunt in the background. Jasmine slid across the liquor-stained floor, crawling as fast as she could to the door. Her hand slipped on the handle, but the guttural cry from behind spurred Jasmine to try again. This time, she was able to rip the door open and came face first with a naked torso. Her eyes traveled up slowly, taking in Jafar with his hand up to knock on the door. His entire body stiffened as he took in Jasmine's disheveled appearance, the way her sleeping gown rode up high on her thighs, then to the room behind her.

Jasmine thought she had seen anger grace Jafar's face before, but nothing compared to the way his face twisted in fury. "Guards!" Jafar bellowed as he wrapped his arm around Jasmine's waist, pulling her to her feet.

"No!" Aladdin screamed as the guards rushed past her and into their room. "I won't let you do this. He's manipulating her. Jafar still wants the throne. Throw *him* back in the dungeon!"

The guards hesitated, and Jasmine stared in shock at her husband. "Take him to the dungeon." Her voice slid from her mouth unbidden, and it felt surreal. Aladdin, the man she loved and thought loved her back, sought to ruin her kingdom. She was surrounded by snakes, alone in her own palace. The guards grabbed Aladdin by his arms, pushing him out the door, and as he neared, Aladdin snarled and spat in her face. "I never liked you anyways, naïve bitch. You weren't even a good fuck."

Jafar jerked Jasmine back, his grip on her waist and across her chest tight, and she collided with his bare skin. Heat engulfed her entire body and Jasmine flinched as the door shut, leaving her all alone with Jafar. "Did all the guards just leave?"

"I do believe so. I don't hear anyone beyond the doors."

Jasmine's breath hitched. "Are you going to finish what Aladdin attempted?"

Jafar's chest rose as he took a deep breath, and his voice grew low. "What exactly did he try to do?"

Jasmine glanced at the bed, then to the balcony, as the breeze ruffled the bottom of the drapes. "I think he was..." She continued staring at the gauzy drapes moving in the breeze, replaying Aladdin's words and actions in her head. "I think... if he wasn't so inebriated..." She turned, gazing into Jafar's eyes. "Why would he..." Jasmine was too upset to finish her sentence.

Jafar let out a deep rumble, his chest vibrating against hers. He reached down, his fingers grazing across Jasmine's thigh. Her stomach clenched, confusion racing through her mind. She briefly felt a tug, and the hem of her dressing gown slid, falling back into place right above her knees. "You are young, and a man took advantage of you and your heart. That is why. He wanted off the streets, and you were an easy target."

Jasmine's chest tightened and she took a step back, eyes still locked with his. "And what about you... what do you want?"

Jafar shrugged. "I'm not a good man, my Sultanah. I want the same thing as I always did. Your kingdom. I probably would have taken you as my wife later on, but I would have never done *this*." He motioned with his hand, pointing to the shattered glass and broken desk behind her. "There are other, more pleasurable ways to put a woman back in her place."

Jasmine pointed to the door. "Get out. I no longer need you for my council."

Jafar's lips lifted in a sinister smile. "No, you don't need me. But you will want me in your corner come time for negotiations tonight. You, a little girl, alone in a den of vicious men who only want one thing from you."

Jasmine lifted her chin as Jafar closed the small distance she had put between them. "And what is that? To fuck me and take my kingdom?"

Jafar's hand slipped behind her neck, holding Jasmine in place. Then he lowered his head, lips almost touching hers. "Yes," he breathed into her mouth and closed the distance, lips covering hers. His kiss was vicious, hard, and he parted her lips with his tongue, tangling it with hers. He broke the kiss just as suddenly as he gave it, leaving Jasmine panting as he took a step back. "I'll wait for you in the throne room tonight. We will reclaim your kingdom, and then I will take it away from you another day."

Jafar stalked away, abandoning Jasmine among broken glass and the ruin of her relationship strewn all around her. She sank to the floor, fingertips lifting slowly to touch her lips. She didn't like the way her mind raced, bouncing between terror, hatred, pain, and lastly, lust for the man who admitted exactly what he wanted from her.

She was in serious trouble.

Chapter Five

JASMINE TOOK A LONG time getting up from the floor, finally picking her way through the glass, tipping the chair back up to standing, and glanced around. The sun was still high in the sky, hours away from the time she would be meeting with the emissary. She sat on the bed and scrubbed her fingertips against her lips again. Her thoughts skittered to Jafar, then to Aladdin. She should probably speak to him now that he had time to sober up.

She stood, shedding her robe and dressing gown. Then she picked out a comfortable tunic and soft, loose pants in light blue before reaching up to re-braid her disheveled hair. Heading towards the door, her hand hesitated on handle, and tears threatened to fall, chest aching. It felt like her heart was breaking open. Before today, she was barely hanging on, and now... now she was drowning. She wasn't fooling anyone.

Which only left her with one choice if she wanted to make sure her kingdom didn't sink with her. Jasmine turned and snatched up her crown. She didn't place it on her head, instead gripping it tightly in her hand as she stalked out of the room. She ended up in front of Jafar's door and yanked it open. He looked up, surprise briefly flickering across his features before standing. Jasmine threw the crown on his bed. "It's yours. I can't do this. I'm done. I have failed in every way. You win."

Jafar's face twisted, a snarl prominent on his lips as he stalked forward and gripped Jasmine's arms, pushing her roughly against the door. "Are you giving me your throne, Jasmine?" His voice was low, their faces almost touching.

"It's what you wanted," she whispered, her defeated gaze dropping to the ground.

Jafar grabbed her chin and lifted, thumb pressing into her lower lip. "No, what I want is to take the throne from a Sultanah. Not have it given to me by a broken little girl. Now pull yourself together—"

Jasmine didn't know why she did it, but she bit down, shutting him up mid-sentence. Her tongue flicked across the pad of his thumb, and she locked eyes with his. "I'm not a little girl," she murmured, opening her mouth to allow him to remove his finger.

Instead, Jafar growled, pushing his body into hers. "You cannot handle me, Jasmine. Do not—"

"Do not presume you know what I can handle."

Jafar's jaw ground down and he bit out his next word. "Fine." Slipping his hand up the base of her neck and into her hair, he grabbed a handful. The pressure from his grip had Jasmine tilting her head back, and an involuntary gasp left her lips. Jafar's chest pressed against hers, locking Jasmine in place against the door as his other hand snaked down the front of her pants. Heat painted her cheeks as his thumb, moments earlier having been in her mouth, slid down the apex of her curls and found its prize. Jasmine's breath hitched, eyes closing as he slid his thumb across her clit and started to circle it.

"Open your eyes," Jafar's rough voice whispered in her ear, as he twisted his hand and slid a finger into her already throbbing and wet pussy. Jasmine let out a little gasp at the sudden intrusion and snapped her eyes open to his command. She locked eyes with Jafar's as he leaned his head down. He stopped, lips scraping against hers, keeping the rhythm with his finger as he slid another inside and pressed his thumb against her clit. A pressure Jasmine had never felt before pooled deep inside. "Tell me," he whispered against Jasmine's lips, "did Aladdin ever fuck you like this?"

Jasmine opened her mouth, just as the pressure broke, cascading through her whole body, and she cried out. Her pussy clenched around Jafar's fingers as he took her bottom lip into his mouth and bit down. Her entire body jerked in pleasure and Jafar slipped his hand out of her pants to tug at the laces, loosening them. He clamped his hand against her hip, fingers still wet from being inside her. His grip in her hair tightened, and he asked again. "Answer me."

Jasmine swallowed, heart burning across her cheeks, but met his eyes. "I've never felt anything like that before."

Jafar's chuckle rasped against her skin as he leaned down, teeth nipping at her exposed neck. "You poor little girl. Married to a man who couldn't even give you an orgasm."

Jasmine hissed, "If that was it, then I think I can handle you just fine, Jafar."

Jafar stilled against her before his laugh rang out, breaking the sudden silence. "Oh, my sweet, naïve Sultanah. I haven't even started with you yet."

In response, Jasmine rolled her hips against his. "Then I suggest you get started."

Jafar crushed his mouth against hers, the kiss deep enough to steal her breath away, and Jasmine's nails sank into Jafar's broad back. He pushed harder into her, grinding her back into the door before breaking the kiss.

She sucked in a lungful of air as Jafar grabbed her pants and ripped them down to her ankles.

Jasmine made a step to lift her foot, but Jafar didn't wait, instead grabbing her by the waist and lifting her higher up against the door. She let out a startled cry that turned into a gasp as Jafar buried his head between her thighs. Her legs hitched over his shoulders, pants falling free to the floor as strong hands gripped her ass and Jasmine cried out again, head falling back as Jafar's tongue slid inside of her.

She buried her hands in his hair, nails scrapping against his scalp as Jafar feasted on her. Jasmine's eyes rolled back in her head as her entire body tightened, waves of pleasure cascading from her core. They rolled through her body, her moans getting higher and higher until they turned into cries.

Slowly, Jafar lifted his head from between her thighs and Jasmine's legs slipped from his shoulders. The second her feet touched the ground, her legs buckled, knees hitting the floor and putting Jasmine exactly where she wanted to be. Grasping her tunic, she shimmied out of it and threw it to the side. Grabbing the ties to Jafar's pants, she loosened them just enough for his erection to spring free.

Jasmine glanced up as Jafar slid his hand through her hair, pulling it away from her face and fisting it in his hand. He stared down at her, his other hand splayed out on the door. A wicked smile formed on Jasmine's lips as she parted them, and with her eyes still locked with

Jafar's, she licked his cock from base to tip. He released a low growl, head tipped back as Jasmine slipped her mouth around his tip and flicked her tongue back and forth, before circling it fully.

She hummed in the back of her throat as she let his shaft slide all the way down until she gagged. "*Fuck*," Jafar breathed out as Jasmine slipped her hand around the base of his cock and began to move up and down. Mouth in tandem with her hand, Jasmine sucked and licked until Jafar's grip on her hair pulled her mouth away. She let out a soft cry, not having finished with him yet, but promptly shut her mouth as Jafar took a step back, forcing her to crawl forward with him.

He took another step and another, until the backs of his legs hit the bed. Jasmine crawled with him, standing when he pulled her up by her hair. As he loosened his grip, Jafar grabbed Jasmine by the waist, stepping behind her. He pushed the weight of his body against her back, a thigh spreading her legs, and his hand wrapped around the back of her neck.

"Get down on your hands and knees." Jafar's voice was thick and hoarse, his command causing Jasmine's pussy to tighten in anticipation. She did as he bid and her moan bit out as the bed dipped, hands tightening around her hips. His cock was thick, stretching her far more than Aladdin's ever did as he took her in one hard thrust.

A scream of pleasure ripped from her throat as Jafar slammed into her from behind, filling her over and over again. His body suddenly covered hers, hand tightening around her throat. She let him pull her back, their position changing, deepening the depth of his cock inside of her. Jafar sat on his haunches, Jasmine straddling his legs, his chest flush with her back. She moaned low, head falling, and Jafar's face filled her vision. His hand still rested around her throat, the other arm around her rib cage right below her breasts. His hand twitched up, fingers twisting around a nipple as he moved his hips in tandem, grinding deep inside of her.

Jasmine cried out again, and Jafar covered her mouth with his, swallowing her cries of pleasure. His tongue thrust deep inside, fucking her mouth in the same manner as his cock. Her entire body shook, waves of ecstasy crashing through her. Jafar broke the deep kiss with a growl, pulling away as his body stiffened, arms tightening around Jasmine. He sighed deeply before loosening his hand across her throat and reached down, grabbing the crown Jasmine had tossed towards the bed earlier.

He thrust it into her hands and whispered, "Don't forget this when you leave. And don't ever offer me your kingdom again, because next time, I will take it. Then you will learn how bad of a man I truly can be."

Jasmine stared at the crown in her hands as Jafar slid out of her and stood. She glanced at him, eyes wide with disbelief at what she had just done, and Jafar threw a wicked smile her way as he tightened the laces to his trousers. He turned without a word and left his room, slamming the door behind him.

Chapter Six

JASMINE STARED AT THE door, cradling her crown in her hands. Her thoughts were a whirlwind. She couldn't believe what she had just done. It was as if someone else entirely had possessed her and she realized it was grief. She was completely lost and alone in the world, in her palace, and she ran right into the arms of a traitor. And why?

It was because she knew exactly what he wanted. Jafar had never lied to her. He might have had a hidden agenda before the ill-fated coup that landed him in the dungeon, but he wasn't hiding anymore. Jasmine shifted, looking to the open balcony, and her eyes widened. The sun was getting low in the sky. She and Jafar had been going at it for hours. Jasmine scrambled from the bed, only to drop to her knees. Her body was sore in places it never had been before, and she thought back to Jafar's words. *You can't handle me, Jasmine.*

She shook his voice from her mind and headed to the door, picking up her pants and tunic on the way. Jasmine's muscles groaned as she donned her clothes and paused to smooth down her hair well enough to place her crown on.

Straightening the tunic, she rolled her shoulders back and stepped out of Jafar's room, only to run into a startled worker about to knock. She bowed low and Jasmine nodded. "It is empty. You can clean if that is what you are here for." She glanced at the large basket in her hands, overflowing with bottles and rags. "Once you are done here, can you send for someone to clean my quarters. It is a bit of a mess."

The lady nodded as Jasmine turned on her heel and made her way down the corridor towards the palace bathing rooms. The guard manning Jafar's door trailed behind her slowly, and she turned to look over her shoulder. "Why are you following me?"

The guard hesitated mid-step. "Jafar ordered us to always have a guard on you. Especially after this morning's incident."

Jasmine stopped and slowly turned. "What were his exact words?"

The guard gulped. "His exact words were, *'There is to be a guard on your Sultanah at all times unless she is in her council's presence. I will not have this kingdom fall to ruin before I'm ready to take it from her hands.'*"

Jasmine stared at the guard, absolutely flabbergasted. "And where is my council at present?"

"Right behind you."

The words didn't echo from the guard's mouth, but from a low voice that sent a shiver down her spine. Jasmine turned to face Jafar. He stood before her, fully dressed in an ornate tunic as black as his hair, stopping at his calves with a slit going up both sides ending near his hips. The pants he wore were loose enough to move in but tapered at his ankles and just as dark as the tunic. The only color was stitching in a dark red. Even the laces and buttons were black. Jasmine's eyes snapped up to his face, freshly shaved, and the upper half of his hair was pulled back in a small bun. "Where are your guards, Jafar?"

He lifted his upper lip in a smirk. "Don't worry, my Sultanah. I won't make any dastardly plans to take your throne. I'll do that after we send the Northern Emissary and his entourage home to lick their wounds."

Jasmine pointed to the guard behind her. "He will stay with you."

Jafar took a step in, invading her space, but instead of stepping away, she glared at him. His smirk broadened. "Then pray tell, who will be your escort to the bathing rooms. I assume you are headed that way?"

"I can walk myself."

Jafar stared her down, but Jasmine didn't avert her gaze. His eyes lingered on her face before glancing at the guard behind her. "We will all walk together, then."

Jasmine opened her mouth to protest before snapping it shut. Stepping around Jafar, she continued down the hall. Jafar turned and glided beside her, barely making a sound, hands clasped behind his back. Jasmine glanced at him from the side, taking him in the best she could while still watching her step. She wanted to say something... *anything* to acknowledge what they had just done, but didn't know how to start up the conversation, nor did she really want the guard to overhear.

Jasmine's face suddenly flushed. The guard probably *did* hear everything. After all, they had been right up against the door. She gulped, heat flaming her cheeks. What seemed like an eternity later, but was only a minute, they stopped in front of the doors leading to the bathing rooms. Jasmine turned, glancing at Jafar and the guard. "I'm pretty sure I can take it from here, unless you wanted to watch me wash myself?" She directed those last words to Jafar with enough menace as she could muster. The guard went rigid and averted his eyes, trying to pretend he wasn't there.

"Such a lovely invitation, my Sultanah, but I think I will have to pass this time around," Jafar murmured and lifted his hand, pushing a loose lock of Jasmine's hair behind her ear. Then he leaned in to whisper, "We need to make sure you can walk into the throne room on your own two feet in an hour."

Jasmine felt her stomach drop as the inside of her upper thighs grew warm and she jerked away from his touch. "You have a high opinion of yourself," she tried to snarl, but her words came out a little too breathy for her liking. Jafar smirked and Jasmine turned as fast as she could, pushing open the door before slamming it behind her.

Humid air and steam billowed into her face, the smell of eucalyptus and mint overwhelming. Jasmine took a hasty look around, but she was fully alone in the chambers. With a relieved sigh, she made her way over to the biggest bath in the far corner. Pulling the long curtains around for privacy, she quickly shed her clothing and crown, stepping fully into the steaming water.

Letting her head fall back, Jasmine threaded her hand through her hair, lathering it with foaming soap and oils. The water moved slightly with her movement, rolling against the tender flesh between her legs. She moaned and cracked her eyes open slightly. There were no sounds except that of lapping water, and she closed her eyes once more before sliding a hand between her legs.

The hazy image of a man dressed in all black rose to her mind's eye as her fingers found her clit. She gasped, thinking back to a very different hand that had been between her legs only hours ago. The man in her mind knelt behind her with an all-knowing smirk cutting across his face. She imagined her hand as his as he leaned over her, heat pooling low down in her core, and she let out another shocked gasp as she came suddenly by her own hand.

Jasmine snapped her eyes open, looking around, but she was still alone in the bath. Letting out a shuddering breath, she quickly finished washing herself. Wrapping a towel around her hair, she dried it into a less wet mess and wiped off her body before donning a thick robe.

Crown once again on her head, Jasmine made her way to the door and steadied herself. The last thing she wanted was to see Jafar and instantly blush from what she had done in the bath. Schooling her face to impassiveness, she pulled open the door, only to be greeted by a completely different guard and a lady-in-waiting. Jafar was nowhere in sight. Jasmine couldn't figure out if she was disappointed or glad.

"Princess?" the lady-in-waiting asked.

"Sultanah... my title is Sultanah. Please remember that." It felt weird correcting her, but Jasmine stood her ground and stared at the lady-in-waiting.

"Sultanah, I apologize," she murmured and curtsied slightly. "We are to escort you to your chambers. Then I am to get you ready for your meeting tonight."

Jasmine nodded and strode down the hallway without another word. Guard and lady-in-waiting trailing quickly behind her.

Chapter Seven

JASMINE STARED AT THE large doors in front of her, Jafar standing slightly behind and to the side. She glanced at him and cleared her throat. "Any advice from my council?"

Jafar leaned on his heels, hands clasped behind his back. Jasmine remembered this pose, the one he usually took when deep in thought. His words were slow in the making. "Do what you feel is right, my Sultanah. I will interject when needed."

Jasmine nodded, reaching for the door until Jafar tsked at her and motioned to the guard. "The Sultanah never opens her own doors."

Her hand dropped as the guard scrambled to open the door. Once open, Jasmine took a deep breath and strode through, Jafar following closely behind. Her eyes roamed to the Northern Emissary and his men. Most of them lounged in the chairs, shirts untucked and raised glasses filled with red liquid to each other. Only the head of the emissary sat upright in his chair, lips drawn in a tight line when he glanced her way, then his eyes flickered to Jafar.

"Gentlemen..." the emissary hummed, raising a hand to his men. "We have a lady present." Turning his eyes back to Jasmine, she came to the end of the table, and he nodded. "Your husband will not be present, I take it."

"I do apologize for the inconvenience, but he is currently sleeping off his drunken state in the dungeons." Jasmine spoke her words in a cool demeanor. All the men were now staring between her, Jafar, and the emissary.

"Sir, did we miss something?" one of the men asked.

"I was under the impression we had a deal and were signing the papers today," another murmured while looking Jasmine up and down with a sneer.

The emissary cleared his throat. "Sorry, men. It seems like we were misinformed on who holds the throne to this kingdom."

Jasmine lifted her chin. "Fortunately, my husband has no say in the final proceedings within my kingdom. I am the rightful heir, and the throne is fully mine at the end of the day."

Grumbles met with Jasmine's words as she made her way around to the head of the table. About to pull out her chair herself, Jasmine paused as Jafar's hand shot out. He pulled the chair out without a word and Jasmine sat. Then he stayed standing next to her in silence, surveying the table and men.

Jasmine had no idea what he was thinking but had to trust he would intervene if she made a drastic error. Grabbing the papers in front of her, Jasmine plastered a smile to her face, ignoring how half of the emissary's men continued to drink, scowling in her direction. A few even flat out refused to acknowledge she was there. It didn't matter to her, though. What mattered was her dealings directly with the head of the Northern Emissary. Clearing her throat, Jasmine began speaking and prayed she could undo the mess Aladdin had put her in.

Jasmine slumped in her chair as the last of the emissary's men left the throne room for the night. They had gotten nowhere. Negotiations going round and round. And Jasmine had gritted her teeth, shrugging off every underhanded comment about her being a woman. Every insult slid beneath elegant words about her kingdom, and every time they purposely chose to call her everything but her title.

Sultanah... she was a Sultanah and the only one who seemed to call her so was currently standing behind her chair, tapping a finger against the top of it. "Have all meetings gone this way since you have taken the throne?" Jafar murmured.

Jasmine sighed, "Mostly."

Jafar continued to tap the back of her chair in a steady rhythm. "And you are sure war is completely off the table?"

Jasmine's back became rigid, and she slowly turned in the chair to face him. "We are trying to avoid war, Jafar. I want to be a fair and kind ruler like my father was. He dealt with all sorts of diplomats and always came away with the good of the kingdom at the forefront of his negotiations."

Jafar stilled, fingers no longer tapping her chair but gripping it. "You have a very idealistic view of your father and his proceedings."

"And what is that supposed to mean?"

Jafar went back to tapping his finger, and Jasmine had to fight the urge to slap his hand. "It means, I, along with your father's council, did most of the deals and negotiations with the emissaries while your father was sitting on his ass."

Anger filled Jasmine's entire body, and she surged up, pointing her finger into Jafar's face. "Do not speak about my father in such a manner. He was a good man and a good ruler. You were the one who tried and failed, might I add, to take the throne from him. And all for what?

Power? Riches? Conquering distant lands? You never loved this kingdom, not like I do, nor how my father did. Everything was fine until your coup."

Jafar had the audacity to laugh, full and throaty, head thrown back. Jasmine's hand twitched, the urge to slap the man laughing at her growing stronger every second. When he finally stopped laughing and leveled his gaze on her, Jasmine took an involuntary step back. His face was hard, fury radiating from his whole being.

Jafar took a step towards her and reached out his hands, grabbing her upper arms and pulling Jasmine into his space. She went still, heart picking up its pace, and heat pooled into her lower abdomen. Damn it, she was not turned on by the cold and heartless man before her, yet as he leaned down, face coming within inches of hers, Jasmine's lips parted slightly.

"I am fine being the villain in this story, but let's get your facts straight. Your father was barely holding on to his kingdom, and nothing was fine before my coup. I wanted to bring this city into greatness, and if I had to go to war to do so, then at least I had the balls to do it. And don't ever accuse me of not loving this city. I care greatly about her, and I will not let you, a naïve little girl playing at Sultanah, run it into the ground." Jafar took a shaking breath and let go of Jasmine's arms, stepping away. "And while we are on the subject, I didn't do it for the riches or power. I did it because of your mother, and I did it for you."

Jasmine couldn't speak, her mind trying to unravel everything Jafar had just said as she watched him stalk away, leaving her all alone in the throne room.

Jasmine was still replaying Jafar's words in her head as she made her way down the hall, starlight streaming through the windows until she started down the stairs. Lanterns lit the walls, and she thought back to the last time she had gone down to the dungeons only days before. This time, though, she would not be seeking council from the man she came to see. No, she was looking for answers. *I did it because of your mother, and I did it for you.*

Jasmine shook her head, trying to get Jafar's snarling confession out of her mind. She had always seen him as the villain, but now Jasmine knew it wasn't quite that simple. Nothing ever was. She turned to glance at the guard trailing behind her. "I'm going to visit my husband alone, if you don't mind."

The guard looked from her to the one standing outside the cell door. They both shrugged, and the one guarding the dungeon shook out his keys. The sound of the lock grinding, metal grating against metal as the door opened was loud against her ears. "He is chained up, Sultanah, so you should be safe."

Jasmine opened her mouth to tell the guard it was Sultanah, not princess, before she realizing he had used her correct title. "Thank you. I will call out if I need anything."

The guard ducked his head in a short bow as Jasmine made her way inside the dungeon cell. Aladdin sat chained against the wall and her mind superimposed another man briefly overtop of this one. It was like staring into a mirror, the positions, the smell, and...

He suddenly threw his head back, breaking the illusion. "Jassie," Aladdin begged, his eyes frantic. "You're here. Finally, let me out of these chains. You are being deceived. Everything will be alright, just let me out of here. We can defeat him again. Together, just like before." Aladdin pulled on his chains, straining to get closer to her.

Jasmine held up her hand and murmured, "Aladdin, stop." She looked around and settled on sitting on the last step of the stairs. Something deep inside of her twisted in warning and she didn't want to get too close.

"Jassie, princess... my Jasmine. Take these cuffs off me. I promise I'll be more help around the kingdom. You don't have to go to him. We can run the kingdom together if that is what you want."

Jasmine stared at Aladdin in utter disbelief. "Aladdin! You just tried to give away my throne right out from under me. I have been asking for your help for months. Months, Aladdin. And you did not care. You had no care other than spending money and getting inebriated. Do you even remember what you did to me earlier today in our chambers? Do you even know what the punishment is for assaulting a Sultanah? Because I..." Jasmine choked on her tears, not able to finish her words.

Aladdin's chains rattled as he got on his knees, hands clasped in front of him, begging. "I will never do that again. I just lost it. I promise I've never done something like that before, and I'll never do it again. I was just so tired, and I thought I had fixed everything. Then you got so disappointed—"

"Disappointed? Aladdin, you *tried* to give away my kingdom. What else have you been doing behind my back?"

"Nothing, Jassie. I promise it was a moment of weakness. I'll never drink or do opium again. I swear."

Jasmine sighed and put her head in her hands. "What am I going to do with you?"

"Jassie, don't cry. It's fine. I'll smooth things over with the emissary. Then I'll take them out again. They will leave happy, and you will still have your throne."

Jasmine glanced up at Aladdin in shock. "Are you joking right now? You just said moments ago you would never go out drinking or go to a den again. Then you say you will take them out to a bar to smooth things over. How does *that* make sense? And how could I ever trust you not to try something like this again?"

Something vicious flickered briefly across Aladdin's features and a shiver ran down Jasmine's spine. "Jassie, I would have to go drink with them to smooth things over. It's what men do; then once they leave, I'll be sober forever. I swear. For you, I can stay sober."

Jasmine shook her head. "Aladdin, I need to ask you something."

Aladdin paused, a pleading look emanating from his face. The more Jasmine looked at him, the more uneasy she felt. Everything he conveyed seemed fake and over the top. Had he been faking this whole time? "Ask me, Jassie. I'm sure it was just a misunderstanding."

Jasmine took a deep breath. "You screamed at me while trying to drag me toward the bed. You were screaming you weren't going back to the streets. That you would make me sign the agreement so you can continue living as you are in the palace." Aladdin opened his mouth to interject, but Jasmine lifted her hand for silence, and for once, he actually shut his mouth. "I don't need to know how you were going to make me sign something against my will. I can only imagine. Just answer this question... did you marry me to get into the palace and off the streets?"

Aladdin's lip trembled slightly. "Jassie, is that what Jafar told you? He is brainwashing you. He wants your throne. He will do anything to get it. I will even forgive you for sleeping with him."

Jasmine blinked slowly. "Excuse me?"

"I forgive you for sleeping with Jafar. I overheard the guards speaking about how you went to his chambers. Jassie, you don't need to be embarrassed. I'm sure you didn't want to. We can put him back down here and forget all of this happened."

Jasmine's mind buzzed. "Royals don't adhere to conventional monogamy. We sometimes must..." she whispered before shaking her head. "No. Stop evading my question, Aladdin. Did you marry me to get off the streets?"

Aladdin stared at her without answering, and she could see it in his eyes. He was trying to figure out how to avoid or lie to her. She had gotten her answer through his silence. Standing, her arms wrapped around her stomach. She felt sick. "Jassie," Aladdin whispered. "The streets... You don't understand."

"No, I don't understand, but you didn't have to lie to me! You didn't have to make me think you loved me for me!" Jasmine screamed, emotions finally bubbling up too high to hide.

Aladdin surged to his feet, face going red. "I had to! I had to get off the streets and there you were. So desperate to escape your smothering palace life and see the city by yourself. So naïve and willing to fall for the poor street urchin with a nice smile. Do not blame me for seizing an opportunity!"

Jasmine shook her head and took a step back before turning and running from the dungeon. Aladdin's screams echoed as she took the stairs two at a time. She didn't know nor care who saw her running down the hall to her room, tears streaming down her face. Safely behind her doors, she fell to the ground and wept as her heart shattered into a million pieces.

Chapter Eight

SHE DIDN'T KNOW HOW long she stayed on the ground weeping, and even as all the tears stopped, Jasmine only had the strength to push herself up into a sitting position. That was how he found her. Soft steps padding up from behind, presence heavy and menacing.

Jasmine didn't turn, staring at the nothingness in front of her. Numbness engulfed her entire being, and she welcomed it.

Hands gently touched her shoulders, but Jafar didn't say anything. He was just a warm presence behind her. She slowly blinked and what felt like an eternity later, she forced words from her mouth, throat dry and cracking. "What am I supposed to do?"

Jafar's hands tightened around her shoulders slightly before releasing once more. "You get up and embrace the pain."

Jasmine tilted her head back, eyes gazing up at Jafar's face. He wasn't looking down at her but forward, to the dark sky above and the stars dancing across the velvet sky. "Is it going to be like this forever?"

Jafar let out a low sigh. "Yes."

Jasmine wasn't expecting such a short response, and she blinked before scowling. "That's it. Just yes? No other wise words from my council."

Jafar finally glanced down, and Jasmine flinched as his hard eyes met with hers. He slowly kneeled, hands trailing down her arms until he was face to face with her. "You want some hard truths, Jasmine. Here is one for you. Start acting like a fucking Sultanah and get up. Steel that spine and harden your heart. You can't have love and your kingdom. You must choose one or the other."

"Why do I have to choose?" Her voice was a whisper, and Jafar chuckled softly. He grabbed her chin in his hand, cupping it.

"Because you will always be put in this same situation, every single time. Them or your crown. That is a hard truth. There is no fairytale ending. No happily ever after."

"No heroes or villains," Jasmine whispered. "Only power and those who wield it."

"Exactly. Now get up and show me exactly who holds power in this kingdom." Jafar dropped his hand from her chin and reached lower, fingers dipping to her waist.

"What—" Jasmine bit off her sentence as Jafar grabbed the waistline of her skirt and shifted to stand, lifting her up with him. He spun her around, hand still holding tight and shuffled her back, pushing yet keeping her close.

"Show me who is in charge here, Jasmine," Jafar rumbled, pushing her back until Jasmine's knees hit the bed and she buckled. Jafar let her fall, his hand moving to the ties on his pants. Face flushing, Jasmine scrambled back onto the bed and sat up on her knees.

"I'm in charge."

Jafar reached out, grabbing Jasmine by her neck and pulled her close. His breath mingled with hers. "I said show me, not tell me."

Jasmine tried to close the distance, but Jafar pushed her back once more. She bit out a frustrated snarl and sat up. Jafar dipped his weight down on the bed, pants loosened and hanging precariously on his hips. As he crawled forward, Jasmine's mouth went dry and heat pooled between her thighs. Jafar reached forward, collaring her throat with his hand, bringing his face close, his body starting to cover hers. Jasmine's eyes fluttered, her head falling back as his knee slowly shoved her thighs apart, her skirt bunching up around her thighs. His lips scrapped against hers. "I guess I am in charge, then."

Jasmine's eyes snapped open at his words. "No, you're not," she breathed out and grabbed Jafar just as he had her. Hand wrapping around his throat, she closed the distance between their lips, tongue tangling with his. He pushed into her, grabbing her wrist and forcing her hand from his neck. Releasing his hold on her neck, he gripped Jasmine's other hand tangled in his hair. He straddled Jasmine's waist, locking both of her hands over her head with his one. She huffed and glared at the smirking man above her. "This isn't fair," she murmured as Jafar's free hand slipped down between her thighs, fingers teasing around her entrance.

He leaned down and whispered in her ear, hands tightening as she twisted, trying to free herself. "Life rarely is fair."

Jasmine turned her head and clamped her teeth down onto Jafar's exposed neck just as he sank a finger inside of her. He let out a low rumble, adding another finger as Jasmine cried out in pleasure, releasing her bite on him. Her hips rose, matching his pace between her thighs, and she twisted her hands again, trying to break his grip. "Should I give you a reprieve, little girl?" Jafar growled, and Jasmine turned her face, tilting her chin up so she could stare him in the eyes.

"It's Sultanah, not little girl," she snarled in his face before taking a shuddering breath as Jafar added his thumb into the mix, circling her clit. "And I don't need a reprieve. I'm ordering you to let go of my wrists."

Jafar immediately released his grueling grip at her command and sank his hand into her hair, mouth clashing with hers. He pulled back slightly. "Good girl. Now show me what else you got."

Jasmine shoved her hands into Jafar's shoulders, forcing him to roll back. His fingers slipped from her, and she almost released a groan from the loss but held it back, barely. Straddling him, she reached down, loosening the ties to her skirt. Shimming out of it, she sat her weight back down on top of Jafar, who was still fully dressed, those damn pants somehow still hanging onto his hips.

"Take this off," Jasmine ordered, hand gripping his tunic, already working the buttons open. Instead, Jafar gave her a wicked smirk and reached up, tucking his hands behind his head.

"Make me," he murmured, and Jasmine grumbled, ripping at the buttons until she finally exposed his chest. Her nails raked down his chest, leaving dark welts behind, and he rose with her rough touch. Reaching to his shoulders, she pulled the tunic from him and threw it across the room. She was breathing hard, chest rising and falling heavily.

Pushing Jafar back down, he didn't fight her this time and instead grabbed her thighs with his hands. "Come up here," he murmured, and Jasmine paused as his hands tightened, trying to force her farther up his chest and to his face. Realizing exactly what Jafar wanted her to do, she let him pull her into position and Jasmine laid her hands on the wall, unsure if she should just hover or sit fully.

Jafar took control, wrapping his arms around her waist, bringing her exposed and pleasure swollen flesh down on his face harder than she would have dared. Jasmine threw her head back with a sharp cry of ecstasy as Jafar's mouth went to work, his tongue slipping in and out of her, flicking up to tease her clit. Her hips rocked to his pace and Jasmine rode Jafar's face, until the pressure building deep inside of her broke and she tightened around his tongue. Jafar slid his tongue out slowly, the tip flicking her clit, and Jasmine let out a low gasp, hands falling from the wall to thread through Jafar's hair.

She shifted slightly, sliding her body down his until his length nestled between his thighs. Jafar reached down, pushing at his pants just enough to free himself before reaching back up and threading a hand behind Jasmine's neck and into her hair. She brought her face down, lips hovering over Jafar's, and licked them, tasting herself on his mouth. He murmured softly, "Finish it, Jasmine."

She sank down, his hard length nudging at her entrance, and Jafar shifted, thrusting into her. It was slow and teasing, and Jasmine moaned into Jafar's mouth as his free hand trailed down to grab her ass, moving her with his pace.

His breath quickened, and Jasmine bit down on his lower lip. A moan, low and throaty, filled the air as Jasmine released his lip, nibbling down his jaw and neck.

His fingers squeezed her ass, pace quickening, and Jafar's grip in Jasmine's hair tightened. She gasped as Jafar thrust deep and ground his hips against hers. Bringing her lips back up to his mouth, Jasmine swallowed his next moan as he went rigid. As Jafar's body relaxed around her, Jasmine broke the kiss to whisper, "I win."

Jafar tightened his arms around her body, keeping her flush with him, and let out a shuddering breath. "Fuck."

Jasmine smiled at his breathless word and trailed her hand up his chest, fingertips grazing across his collarbone before she gently wrapped her hand around his throat. "Now address me as your Sultanah and fuck me again."

Jafar's rasping laugh echoed through the darkness as he removed Jasmine's hand from his throat and rolled, crushing his body over hers. "Yes, my Sultanah," he murmured before leaning down and taking her mouth with his.

JASMINE WOKE WITH A start, pre-dawn light streaming through the open curtains. Rolling over, she clutched the sheets to her chest and paused, taking in the man standing on the balcony overlooking the city. Slipping from the bed quietly, Jasmine donned her robe and padded out to meet him. As she came closer, her eyes snagged upon his bare back and Jasmine paused mid-step. Scars, some light and others so deep the tissue was still raised, crisscrossed almost every inch of his back. Starting from the bottom of his shoulder blades all the way down to where his pants hung low on his hips. Jasmine took a step closer, hand outstretched, as Jafar turned. She met his searching eyes, and anger hardened her face. "Who did that to you?"

Jafar's gaze slipped away from hers, and he turned to look back over the city. "They are old. From another life."

Jasmine took a step closer, hand settling right between his shoulder blades. "That wasn't what I asked, Jafar."

"It's of no concern, Jasmine. Don't think that because we fuck each other, you should care about me. It's cute but not needed."

Jasmine's hand fell from his back, only to reach up and grab his shoulder, pulling him towards her. "Stop being a prick and answer me. And don't tell me who I should care about and why. Now, tell me, who did that to you."

Jafar shook his head, but leveled his gaze with hers. "Just remember you asked, because you are not going to like the answer. During your father's early rule, there was a law, and it didn't matter if you were a child or adult, male or female. It applied to all. Any disrespect towards a guard patrolling the city and your punishment was fifty lashings." Jasmine gulped, realizing what Jafar was saying. She tried to look away, but he grabbed her chin, keeping her eyes on his face. "I was ten, homeless, living on the streets, and I accidentally bumped into a guard running away from a gang of kids. I was left on the lashing post for three days."

Jasmine's eyes began to water, and she whispered, "This isn't a law anymore."

Jafar let go of her chin and pushed a loose piece of hair behind her ear. "No. Your mother saved me from that day and demanded your father strike the law from record. She was also the one who insisted I live in the palace and learn a trade. She was a good woman. Gentle, but when needed, she was an unmovable mountain. Your father never deserved her."

Jasmine shook her head. "I didn't know you knew her so well. I only have snippets of memories of her."

Jafar took a deep breath and reached out, caressing her lips with his thumb. "Don't fall for me, Jasmine. I will never be a good man," he murmured before pulling away and walking around her.

She turned, watching him shrug his tunic back on and head for her door. Hand on the handle, he turned and met her gaze, dark hair falling into his eyes. "I'll meet you in the throne room. Remember to show the emissary exactly who holds the power here. Because if you don't, I will take that crown from you."

Jasmine took a step forward, crossing her arms and lifting her chin. "Do not threaten me, Jafar."

His lips lifted into a smirk as he opened the door. "Don't give me a reason to."

The door closed with a snick and Jasmine exhaled a low breath before striding over to her wardrobe and flinging the doors open. Jafar was right. It was time to show the Northern Emissary exactly who wielded the power in her kingdom. And how far she was willing to go to keep it.

Chapter Nine

SHE TOOK A DEEP breath and flung open the doors to her chamber. Zeroing in on the two guards, Jasmine approached one and gave him an order. He hesitated and glanced at the other guard.

"You will do as you are ordered," Jasmine said before turning on her heel and continuing down the palace corridor, not even looking over her shoulder to see if the guard obeyed her. Her tunic fluttered around her legs as Jasmine's strides got shorter, and she stopped in front of the closed doors to the throne room. She could hear the voices from the emissaries inside, laughing and growing louder by the second.

Glancing to the mirror on the wall, she reached up and tucked away a stray hair. Normally, she kept it back in a half style, flowing down her back like a waterfall or in a long braid, but not today. Instead, she had wrapped it around her head, weaving it artistically along her crown. Jasmine took in the rest of her outfit, dark red in color, with black stitching along the tunic and down the sides of her pants. They were loose and flowing, tapering at the ankle. Slits along the sides going all the way to her upper thighs. It was something she had never thought of wearing before, completely casual instead of formal. Except she was the Sultanah here, and she chose what she wanted to wear. The color was one she had never worn before either, and it brought out the color of her heritage. Dark tan skin and almond eyes stared back at her. She felt and looked like a goddess of old, a flame raging against darkness, cutting down all who sought to oppose it.

Lifting her chin, she nodded to the guard. He pulled the door open for her, and she drifted into the room. Head held high, she didn't bother looking to see who was present. The voices died down as Jasmine skirted the table she normally sat at and took the three stairs up to the dais. Turning, she landed heavily on the seat of her throne. Her eyes roamed the room, finally taking in everyone before her. Jasmine slowly crossed her legs, and her gaze lingered on Jafar. "My council will join me on the dais. Everyone else will be seated."

Jafar raised an eyebrow, gaze skimming her body before obeying her command and meeting her on the dais. He placed himself on her left side, hands clasped behind his back. Jasmine didn't spare him another glance and instead stared at the Northern Emissary and his men. All of whom were sitting except one. The head of the emissary took a step forward, his gaze skimming up her legs and finally settling on her chest with a sneer. "You look exquisite today, my lady."

Jasmine gripped the arms of her throne and glowered down at him. "You will address me as Sultanah, or I may allow Queen, as is the common title in your country. And if I remember correctly, I told you to *sit*." Her voice rang out sharp and biting. "But if you prefer, you may kneel instead. One or the other, because your disrespect stops now."

The emissary met her eyes quickly, searching Jasmine's face for any hint of weakness before glancing at Jafar, then back to her. "My apologies, Sultanah," he murmured before bowing and turning, taking a seat at the table.

"Now... I am done playing this game. We will reenact the same contract your king had in place with my father. If this is not something you are authorized to do, then tell your king I will await his presence here in my kingdom. If he chooses to push back, you will tell him the following. I will close the borders immediately to your trade caravans. You will no longer be using my city as a through route. We do not need anything from your country or your king. Do I make myself clear?"

The emissary opened his mouth in shock just as the guard Jasmine ordered earlier arrived. With him, he dragged a chained man, stopping at the entrance of the throne room. Jasmine raised her hand, beckoning him to come closer. "Just on time. As a gift, I will give you this traitor, since you seem to get along so well."

Jasmine got up, taking a step forward, and locked eyes with the shackled man on his knees, gaping up at her. "As Sultanah, I officially void our marriage contract. In the past, this would be a death sentence, but I am feeling merciful. You will leave with the Northern Emissary and keep your life."

Aladdin tried to surge to his feet, but the guard kept him on his knees. "Jasmine! You can't do this—"

Jasmine snapped her fingers and pointed at the guard. "Gag him." Aladdin suddenly became muffled, and Jasmine turned to address the emissary once more. "Do we have a deal, or do you need to speak to your king?"

The emissary looked to his men before glancing back to Jasmine. "I will need to bring your request back to the king. We were not given the option to reenact the contract your father previously had between the two kingdoms."

Jasmine sat back on her throne and lifted her hand in a dismissive manner. "You will leave tonight. If you are found lingering after dusk, you will be thrown into the dungeons. Then your king and I will be having an entirely different conversation. And don't forget your gift." She threw a soft, venomous smile at the emissary, and his men gaped at her.

Jafar took a step forward, placing a hand on the top of her throne. "You heard the Sultanah. You are dismissed. To make sure you adhere to her orders, the guards will escort you to your rooms and outside the city limits."

They slowly stood, bowing one by one before shuffling out of the throne room. The guard holding on to Aladdin dragged him out as he stared at Jasmine wide-eyed. The doors closed, leaving them alone, and Jasmine glanced up to Jafar. His eyes roamed her face before he dropped his hand, once more clasping them behind his back. "I think," he murmured, still staring at her, "that I underestimated you."

Jasmine tilted her head. "I'll take that as a compliment."

Jafar nodded. "It was meant to be one."

Jasmine leaned back, gently tapping at the arm on her throne. "In your opinion, how do you think the king will take my demands?"

"In my opinion, I think you will get them. The king is a pushover."

A small smile touched Jasmine's lips, and she turned to stare at Jafar. "And what about you? Should I still be watching my back?"

"Always," Jafar uttered, "but for the time being, you are safe. From me, at least."

Jasmine licked her lips. "I think I'll keep you around for now. Keep me on the right path. For my kingdom."

Jafar titled his head. "I appreciate that, Sultanah."

Jasmine leaned forward. "How would you like to sit on my throne right now, Jafar?"

Jafar opened his mouth before shutting it, and a wicked grin touched his lips. He stalked forward, leaning down to rest one hand on the arm of the throne, and stroked Jasmine cheek with the back of his other. "It seems to be currently occupied."

Jasmine leaned into his touch, arching her back. "Then remove me," she whispered, voice growing husky.

Jafar dropped his hand to her thigh and slipped it between the slit of her pants. His fingers tightening behind her knee as he lifted her leg, hooking it around his waist. Jasmine grabbed onto his shoulders as Jafar completely invaded her space. He moved his other hand and did the same thing. Once both her legs were snug against his hips, Jafar twisted and Jasmine's grip tightened as he moved, changing their positions. In seconds, he was the one sitting on the throne and Jasmine wiggled in his lap, situating herself along his hard length.

Her stomach dipped in anticipation as his hands released the back of her knees and moved up slowly. She bit out a moan, legs tightening around his waist as his hands rested against her ass. She leaned forward, nipping at his lip, and he let out a rumble.

Jafar slipped his hands out of her pants and grabbed the front of her tunic. Their breath mingled, lips a hair's breadth away from each other's as Jafar's fingers slowly unbuttoned her top. Jasmine went to shrug it off, but he stopped her. Instead, he splayed his hands around her rib cage and dipped his head low, taking a hardened nipple in his mouth. Jasmine gasped and threaded her hands through his hair. His tongue rolled her nipple before teasing it with his teeth. Jasmine whimpered as his other hand, hot to the touch, slid up, squeezing her boob. Teasing her other nipple with his fingers, Jasmine shuddered.

Jafar slowly released her other nipple from his mouth, kissing his way up her chest and neck. Dropping a hand to his waist, she splayed her hand over his hard length. He released a soft hiss as she rubbed up and down slowly.

"Replace your hand with your mouth," Jafar commanded in a whisper against Jasmine's neck. Her hand tightened before slowly releasing and she unlocked her legs, shimmying off Jafar's lap to settle down on her knees. Pulling at the ties of his pants, she freed his erection as Jafar's hand slid around the back of her neck and squeezed.

Dipping her head down, Jasmine licked around his tip, teasing her tongue slowly down his shaft before licking back up to the top. She took him in her mouth, and Jafar sighed, hand sliding up her head, fingers teasing through her hair.

"That's a good girl," he murmured, and Jasmine hummed in the back of her throat, teeth scraping up his shaft, and his hand tightened. "Fuck," he breathed out, as Jasmine took his balls in her other hand. Dipping her head low again, she let her teeth scrape harder and tugged on his balls. Jafar's hand tightened even more, gripping her hair and holding Jasmine in place as he growled low.

Pulling her forward, Jafar reached down, untying the strings of her pants. They loosened, falling to her thighs, and Jafar spun her around, pulling Jasmine down onto his lap. She let out a hoarse scream of pleasure as his hot length slid into her soaking and throbbing pussy.

Jasmine's spine arched as Jafar's breath teased on her neck and he began to move his hips. She choked on a strangled moan, hands gripping the arms of her throne. The way her pants restricted the widening of her legs made her feel tighter than normal, and as Jafar ground into her from behind, Jasmine shuddered in his arms, her moans becoming breathless screams.

His mouth teased at her neck, making his way up to nip her jaw with his teeth. Spine straightening, her mouth gasped as his hand slid down, brushing over her clit. She shuddered around him just as he released a trembling groan into her ear.

Jasmine collapsed against Jafar, panting and gasping, shudders raking up her spine, legs tangled with his. He held her tight, arms wrapped around her middle, breathing just as hard. She sighed, low and satisfied, as Jafar turned his head, face meeting hers. They stayed that way, holding on to each other until Jafar grew soft, slipping out of her.

"I could get used to this," he murmured.

Jasmine smiled wickedly. "Long live the Sultanah and her kingdom."

Jafar let out a rasping laugh and kissed her deep, echoing Jasmine's words against her lips.

The End

Also By Astrid Vail

Fairytales After Dark
Claiming Jafar
Gaston's Beast
Hunting Red
Wicked Snow
Holidays After Dark
Winter's Eve
Valentine's Arrow
Discover More and Buy Here
eBook and paperback:

https://books2read.com/u/3J6QjP
Visit my website – buy signed paperbacks & swag
www.roguequeenromance.com

About the Author

Fantasy & Paranormal Erotic Romance Author
Storyteller at Heart
Born in the backwoods of California, Astrid Vail was
raised upon fairytales and fantasy worlds.
With a love of everything otherworldly, Astrid decided
to put pen to paper and pull the exotic creatures dancing
in her head out into the light of day.
She has been writing professionally since 2022 and has
no intention of slowing down anytime soon.
Signup to her newsletter at
www.roguequeenromance.com for a free book or two,
cover reveals, and all things related to extra spicy book
news.

Printed in Great Britain
by Amazon

43203517R00046